GW00858152

Hits the Headlines

Fizzy

Hits the Headlines

Michael Coleman

Illustrated by

Philippe Dupasquier

ORCHARD BOOKS

ORCHARD BOOKS
96 Leonard Street, London EC2A 4RH
Orchard Books Australia
14 Mars Road, Lane Cove, NSW 2066
First published in Great Britain 1993
First paperback publication 1994
Text © Michael Coleman 1993
Illustrations © Philippe Dupasquier 1993
The right of Michael Coleman to be identified as the author
and Philippe Dupasquier as the illustrator has been
asserted by them in accordance with the
Copyright, Designs and Patents Act, 1988.
A CIP catalogue record for this book
is available from the British Library.
1 85213 485 2 Hardback
1 85213 518 2 Paperback
Printed in Great Britain

CONTENTS

1

Fizzy in Trouble

"Now, pay attention!" cried Mrs Grimm.

Fizzy groaned. "Looks like another yuk session," she whispered to her friend Maya. Maya giggled.

"Lucy's beautiful singing voice," said their teacher, beaming at the pig-tailed girl standing next to her, "is starting to make her quite famous."

"Beautiful!" hissed Fizzy, "She must be

joking! Our cat's got a better voice than
Lucy Hardwick!"

"Here she is in the *Millington Recorder*,"
said Mrs Grimm, holding up the local newspaper and pointing to a tiny photograph in
one corner of an inside page, "receiving
first prize in last week's Music Festival."

"The judges must have made a mistake,"
whispered Fizzy to Maya. "Maybe they
thought it was a farmyard noises contest."

Maya snorted. Her giggles were starting to get the better of her.

Mrs Grimm looked up. "Quiet!" she shouted. "Maya Sharma, what is the matter with you, girl?"

"Nothing, Mrs Grimm," said Maya, struggling to get her giggles under control.

Mrs Grimm's gaze fixed on Fizzy. "Fiona Izzard, do you know why Maya looks like she's about to burst?"

"No, Mrs Grimm," said Fizzy, wrinkling her nose.

Mrs Grimm folded the newspaper carefully and handed it back to Lucy Hardwick.

"Thank you, dear. I'm quite sure you're going to be famous one day." She looked angrily towards Fizzy and Maya. "Which is more than we can hope for some people!"

Lucy Hardwick took the newspaper with a squeaky "Thank you, Mrs Grimm." Then she trotted daintily back to her seat in front of Fizzy.

"Creep!" hissed Fizzy.

Making sure that Mrs Grimm couldn't see her, Lucy Hardwick poked her tongue out. Then, flicking her two long pigtails carefully over her shoulders, she sat down.

Fizzy couldn't resist it. She gave Maya a nudge. Maya nodded. Moments later, as Mrs Grimm's back was turned, they were leaning forward to grab one pigtail each.

"Now!" hissed Fizzy.

"Eeeeeeeeek!" yelled Lucy Hardwick as she felt her head being pulled off.

"Lucy!" called Mrs Grimm, looking up. "What is the matter, dear?"

Fizzy braced herself. She was going to be in trouble now. And so it proved. But not in the way she expected.

"It was excitement, Mrs Grimm," lied Lucy Hardwick with a nasty smile. "Fiona Izzard just told me that *she's* going to have her picture in the newspaper as well."

Mrs Grimm's eyes widened. "Is she now?"

"No, I didn't!" cried Fizzy.

Mrs Grimm nodded in an I-thought-not kind of way.

"I thought not," she said. "Girls like you, Fiona Izzard, are good for nothing."

That was when Fizzy said it. She was so angry, it just popped out. And from then

on, things went from bad to worse.

"Okay, I did," she said loudly, "I *am* going to have my picture in the newspaper. And on the front page!" she added, getting a bit carried away.

"I *am* impressed," said Mrs Grimm. "Tell me more. Why will you have your picture in the newspaper?"

Fizzy gulped. What could she say? It had to be good. You don't get on the front page for nothing.

But she didn't do anything special. Not really. She was pretty good on the trampoline, but that was it. Oh yes, and she knew the Top Fifty backwards, forwards and upside down, but that wouldn't get her on the front page, would it? Or would it?

The idea hit her suddenly. Before she could stop herself she cried, "I'm going to have my picture taken with Pete Za!"

The effect was amazing. The whole class gasped at once.

"Quiet!" bellowed Mrs Grimm, before turning back to Fizzy. "Pizza who?" she said.

"Pete Za?" said Maya, open-mouthed. "You've never ever heard of Pete Za? Pete Za and the Red-Hot Peppas?"

"No," said Mrs Grimm.

"They're top of the charts, Mrs Grimm."
It was Lucy Hardwick, looking green with
envy and red with anger at the same time.
"And Pete himself is ... " she went all
glassy-eyed " ... just wonderful."

"Mmmm," said Mrs Grimm. "And you're
going to be pictured with him, are you
Fiona?"

"Sure," said Fizzy. "Me and Pete are old
pals."

"Then I look forward to next week's
edition of the *Millington Recorder* with inter-
est," said Mrs Grimm.

Maya grabbed Fizzy just as soon as school
was over.

"I didn't know you'd met Pete Za!" she
squealed. "You never said!"

"That's because I haven't."

"What? So how are you going to get your picture taken with him?"

Fizzy smiled. "Simps! He's coming to Millington tomorrow, isn't he?"

"Of course he is," said Maya. "Everybody knows that!"

The school had been buzzing with the news for weeks. Berkeley's, the biggest store in Millington, were opening a new music department and Pete Za had agreed to perform the opening ceremony.

"So ... " said Fizzy.

"So?" asked Maya doubtfully. When Fizzy started off a sentence with the word "so", it usually meant trouble.

"So ... there's bound to be a photographer there!"

"Billions of them," agreed Maya. Pete Za's blond hair and sun-tanned face had been on the front cover of more magazines and newspapers than she'd had school dinners.

"So ... " said Fizzy, "all we've got to do ... "

"*We?*"

"You want to be in the picture as well, don't you?"

Maya thought for an instant, then nodded. "You bet!"

"So ..." repeated Fizzy, "all we've got to do is get there early so we're at the front.

Then, when Pete cuts the ribbon or what-
ever he's going to do, we nip behind him
and get in the picture. Like I said, simps!"

"You're sure it will work?" said Maya.

"Sure, I'm sure," said Fizzy. "All we've
got to do is get there early."

2

Queue Jumpers

"Oh no!" groaned Fizzy.

For once, Maya didn't ask a question. She just repeated what Fizzy had said the day before: "All we've got to do is get there early!"

"We are early!" cried Fizzy, looking at her watch.

It was only 8 o'clock, and on a Saturday morning – that was mega-early. Even so, a

massive queue was in place outside Berkeley's department store. It stretched all along the store front and right round the corner.

"Look at it!" said Fizzy.

"They could have a picture taking up all the front page," said Maya, "and we still wouldn't get in it."

Fizzy thought hard. They had to get near
the front of the queue. But how?

"There's Nicky," said Maya, pointing to a

girl in the crowd. "And there's Marcine," she said, pointing to another girl a bit further back. "There must be half the school here."

"So . . ." said Fizzy, "so . . . maybe there's somebody we know near the front who'll say they saved us a place!"

There was. But she wouldn't.

Lucy Hardwick was standing almost at the head of the queue, very close to Berkeley's glass front doors and their uniformed doorman.

"Lucy!" said Fizzy as she spotted her. "Lucy, old pal! Thanks for saving us a place!"

Fizzy and Maya tried to elbow their way in beside her, but Lucy Hardwick was having none of it.

"Hey!" she shouted. "Stop pushing in!"

"What's all this then!" It was the uniformed doorman, who'd come over to see what all the fuss was about. "Anyone need first aid?"

"She will," said Lucy Hardwick, pointing at Fizzy, "if she tries pushing in again. She's making out she's my friend and I've never ever seen her before in my life!"

"Oh," said the doorman, whose name was Norman. He looked disappointed. "Nobody needs any first aid then? Pity."

"Why?" said Maya, who liked to get to the bottom of things.

"Just been on a course, ain't I?" said Norman the Doorman.

"Why?"

Fizzy groaned. Who cared why? Why couldn't Maya stop asking questions?

"So that I can care for any of our customers what might happen to be in need of first aid," said Norman. "Which is why," he added with a jerk of a thumb in the direction of Berkeley's front doors, "we have a fully equipped in-store first aid room."

Fizzy's ears nearly stood on end. In-store, he'd said. *Inside* the store.

If she needed first aid she would get inside!

And so, right there, slap-bang in front of Norman the Doorman, Fizzy groaned and moaned and collapsed in a heap.

Laying on the ground with her eyes tightly shut she heard Norman the Doorman's gruff voice say, "'Ere! She's fainted!"

"She has?" It was a question, so it had to be Maya.

"No doubt about it," Fizzy heard Norman say. "Right! Into the first aid room it is."

Fizzy felt herself being scooped up from the pavement and carried along.

"What about me?" asked Maya. "She's my best friend."

"Well, you'd better come too I suppose."

"Hey! What about me? Can I come in as well?"

At the sound of this third voice, Fizzy risked a little peep out of one eye. Lucy Hardwick had jumped out of the queue and was running towards them. Fizzy shut her eye again quickly.

"You?" she heard Norman the Doorman say. "You?"

"She's my friend too," said Lucy Hardwick.

"No she's not," said Norman. "A minute ago you said you'd never seen her before in your life. And," he added, "you've lost your place in the queue now."

Moments later, Fizzy felt herself being carried into Berkeley's department store.

Even through the plate glass doors she could hear Lucy Hardwick's shrill voice pleading to be allowed back into the queue again.

But she, Fizzy, was inside!

Under the same roof as the one and only Pete Za!

It had worked!

Well, as good as.

All she had to do now was escape from Norman the Doorman.

3

A Nut Case?

"Fainting is a serious business," said Norman the Doorman, as he plonked Fizzy down on a lumpy camp bed, "very serious. You can't be too careful with heads."

He opened a cupboard with a red cross on the front. "Now then ..."

With her eyes tightly shut, Fizzy couldn't see what he was doing. But then she didn't have to. Norman named everything as he pulled it out.

"Aspirins, bandages, plasters, stingy stuffy ..."

"She's only fainted," Fizzy heard Maya say. "She'll be all right in a minute. Won't she?"

"Could be," said Norman the Doorman.

He carried on unloading. "Scissors, very sharp knife ... "

Fizzy was getting really nervous. What was he going to do?

"Extra-long twiddly things ... "

"What are you going to do with them!" Fizzy heard Maya cry as Norman pulled a big pair of tweezers from the cupboard.

"Just have a bit of a poke about. She might have some chewing-gum stuck down her throat. Dangerous stuff chewing-gum, if it gets stuck. Remember if she was chewing gum, do you?" Norman asked Maya.

Say no, Maya! thought Fizzy.

"Don't know," said Maya. "She might have been."

Fizzy couldn't stand it any more. She blinked open her eyes.

"No, I wasn't!" she yelled, "and I'm okay now. So if you don't mind," she said, hopping her legs off the camp bed and on to the floor, "we'll be off."

Norman held up his hand. "Just you hold on, young lady. Not so fast. You need checking out."

"I'm fine, I tell you. I just ... er ... fainted, that's all."

"With the excitement, I expect," added Maya helpfully.

Norman the Doorman shook his head sadly. His first-ever patient, and it looked like he was going to have to let her go. Unless ... He tried one more thing.

"What's your name?"

"Eh?" said Fizzy.

"Your name. What's your name?"

"Fi ... " Fizzy stopped. Was it a good idea to give her name? What if – well, she couldn't think of a what if, but it just didn't seem a good idea to say who she was.

"Well?" repeated Norman.

"Er ... " stammered Fizzy. "Er ... it's ... "

"Thought so," announced Norman the

Doorman. "Lost her memory, ain't she? Head troubles. Told you."

"I haven't lost my memory!" exclaimed Fizzy. "My name's ... er ... Lucy Hardwick!"

"No it isn't," said Maya helpfully. "It's Fiona Izzard. Don't you remember?"

"Ha!" Norman the Doorman looked triumphant. "There you are then. I knew I was right."

He pushed Fizzy back on to the camp

bed and marched towards the door.

"What are you going to do?" yelled Fizzy.

"Ring the hospital," said Norman. "Lost memory, bad sign, that is. Could be brain sprain."

He opened the door. "Now don't you move. I'll have an ambulance here in a jiffy."

"You idiot!" yelled Fizzy at Maya as soon as he'd gone. "I only made out I'd fainted to get us in here. Now there'll be a fleet of ambulances on their way in a minute!"

Maya started to panic. "What are we going to do?"

"Move!" yelled Fizzy, hopping off the bed and heading for the door, "as fast as we can!"

4

Bed Time!

"Where are we going?" asked Maya as they ran out of the first aid room.

"Anywhere!" yelled Fizzy. "So long as it's away from here."

Off she charged, down a long corridor and up a flight of stairs. At the top was a door. Fizzy didn't stop. She just opened it and went through.

"Beds," said Fizzy. "Look at them all."

There were beds everywhere. Single beds, double beds, little beds and big beds.

"I think we're in the bed department," said Maya.

"Brilliant," said Fizzy. "But we don't want beds. We want music."

And, suddenly, they got it.

"Listen!" cried Fizzy as a jangle of guitars

and drums started up. "They're playing *Take Me Away!*"

She was right. The sounds of Pete Za's number one smash hit were loud and clear. They seemed to be coming from where the sea of beds ended in a tall screen.

"That must be where the new music department is!" said Fizzy. "Let's go!"

They dashed across the floor, ducking and diving between the beds. The nearer they got, the louder the music got. By the time they reached the final row of beds it sounded really close.

"The music department must be on the other side of this screen," said Fizzy. The screen had pictures on it and was made up to look like an enormous bedroom wall. "All we've got to do is get round the other side and ..."

"How?" asked Maya.

"Easy," said Fizzy. "We just ... Oh, no!"

For once, Maya had asked a good question. The screen ran from one side of the bed department's floor to the other. It didn't have a way round.

"We'll have to go back down the stairs and come up again the other way," said Maya.

"Too late," said Fizzy. Different noises were coming from the other side of the screen now, this time of screams and running feet. "They must have let everybody in," she said. "By the time we get round there we'll be lucky if we can see anything at all."

Suddenly a hush fell over the crowd on the other side of the screen. Something was about to happen.

Then a voice screamed. "It's him!"

"Pete. Oh, Pete!" yelled somebody else.

"Pete, we love you!" cried another.

On their side of the screen, Fizzy and Maya just looked at each other helplessly.

"He must have arrived!" cried Fizzy. "And we're missing him!"

She looked up at the top of the screen. It wasn't that high. "If only we could see over," she said.

"There's nothing to stand on that's tall enough," said Maya. "Just beds."

Fizzy's eyes lit up. Beds! Springy beds! Of course! How many times had she practised her trampolining on her bed at home!

She dashed over to the bed nearest the screen, hopped on it – and started bouncing.

Boing! Boing!

Not high enough.

Boing!! Fizzy just caught sight of the crowd on the other side of the screen before she came down again.

Boing!!!

This time she saw a ribbon, stretched

across the entrance to the new music department.

Boing!!!!

And Pete! She could see Pete Za! Not his face, because he was standing with his back to her waiting to cut the ribbon. But it was definitely him!

Booiing!!!!!!

With one enormous bounce, Fizzy got up high enough to see right over the top of the screen, just as Pete cut the ribbon, the cameras flashed and everybody cheered.

Then a voice she knew shouted, "There she is! That's the one!"

Boing! ... B'doing ... Bong.

Fizzy stopped bouncing as Norman the Doorman's voice cut through the air. Behind him were two large-looking ambulance men carrying a stretcher.

"See," shouted Norman, "she don't know what she's doing! I bet you anything she's got a bruised brainbox!"

"He's right, Don," said the ambulance-man at the front, "she does look a bit funny."

"You're right, Den," said the one at the back, "a job for the head doctors if ever I saw one."

Fizzy didn't have much time.

Boing! As Norman the Doorman made a grab for her Fizzy bounced from the bed she was on across to the huge double bed next door.

Don and Den the ambulancemen now closed in. Don went round one side of Fizzy's bed while Den went round the other side. Luckily for Fizzy both of them forgot to let go of their end of the stretcher.

Crack! They bounced away from the bed and landed groaning in an untidy heap.

Fizzy didn't wait to find out if they were all right.

Boing! Boing! Boing! With Maya close behind she bounced over the beds and out through the door leading to the stairs.

And they didn't stop running until Norman the Doorman, Berkeley's Department Store and Pete Za were far behind them.

5

Going up in the World

Fizzy bent down to tie up her shoelace.

"What, again!" cried Maya. "That must be the billionth time this morning!"

"I can't help it if the thing keeps coming undone, can I?"

"Anyone would think you don't want to get to school early," said Maya as they slowly walked on again.

"I *don't* want to get there early," said

54

Fizzy. "I don't want to get there at all!"

She sighed. It was all right for Maya. She wasn't the one who was going to be hauled out in front of the class and have the *Millington Recorder* waved under her nose by a grim Mrs Grimm wanting to know how come Pete Za's picture was in there and hers wasn't.

"I suppose it'll still be there," said Fizzy.

Maya gave her a look. "Suppose what will still be there?"

"School," said Fizzy. "I mean, it could have got burnt down over the weekend, couldn't it? These things happen, don't they?"

Maya shook her head. "They would have said about it on the news."

She was right. As they turned the corner, Fizzy saw to her disappointment that their school was still standing.

Then she had another thought. "Hey, maybe Mrs Grimm will be away today.

56

D'you reckon? She could have been struck down by something nasty, couldn't she?"

"Like what?" asked Maya.

"I don't know! The 'flu! A bus! Anything!"

"No," said Maya again. She was pointing at the small red car sitting just inside the school gates. "Her car's here already."

Fizzy tried once more.

"Maybe the *Millington Recorder* won't come out today, then. Maybe they'll run out of paper. Or ink. Maybe they'll run out of paper *and* ink. What d'you reckon?"

Maya looked at her. "Do you want an honest answer?"

Fizzy shook her head. "No."

"Just what I was going to say," said Maya, "No."

And she was right. Straight after morning break the class was called to attention.

"I have in my hand," announced Mrs Grimm in her loudest voice, "today's edition of the *Millington Recorder*."

She waved the newspaper above her head. "Fiona Izzard, step forward."

Fizzy left her place and walked, head down, to the front of the class.

When she got there, Mrs Grimm pushed the newspaper under her nose.

"Fiona Izzard. This picture on the front page. Tell the class about it please."

Fizzy read the headlines out loud. "Top star Pete Za opens new music department."

"Now then," said Mrs Grimm loudly. "Who can we see?"

"Pete!" called someone.

"Yes, Mr Za is clearly in the centre of the

picture. So is the store manager. And, all around them, I can see a lot of young people. But nowhere ... NOWHERE," she said loudly, "can I see you, Fiona."

"See," whined Lucy Hardwick, "she was making it up."

"Thank you, Lucy," said Mrs Grimm coldly. "There is also a small picture on page 4 showing a girl being led away by a policeman for trying to jump the queue. That girl is you, Lucy, a matter which I will see you about later. As for now ... " Mrs Grimm turned again to Fizzy, "I am talking to you, Fiona."

"But ... " began Fizzy.

"No buts! In this very room on Friday, you said that you would have your picture in this newspaper. Is that not so?"

"Yes ..." gurgled Fizzy. Her eyes were fixed on the picture on the front page of the *Millington Recorder*.

"And is it?" demanded Mrs Grimm.

Fizzy looked hard at the picture. She blinked and looked once more. "Yes!" she cried. "It is! There!"

And there it was.

Behind Pete Za was a tall screen. And above the screen, caught in the middle of a boing was Fizzy's face.

Mrs Grimm peered closely at the picture. "Good heavens," she cried, "so it is!"

Maya called out, "Fizzy's famous!" and almost everybody cheered.

Only Lucy Hardwick wasn't smiling as Fizzy went back to her place clutching the *Millington Recorder* that Mrs Grimm had allowed her to keep.

"I suppose you think you're very clever," she hissed.

Fizzy tapped the picture.

"The camera never lies, Lucy," she laughed. "So you've got to agree I'm going up in the world!"